THE BIGGEST SPLASH

Thomas Taylor

OXFORD
UNIVERSITY PRESS

One hot day, Clovis was sitting by
the lake doing nothing naughty at all.
Suddenly, he noticed something strange.

For Bob Case, my grandad

OXFORD
UNIVERSITY PRESS

Great Clarendon Street, Oxford OX2 6DP

Oxford University Press is a department of the University of Oxford.
It furthers the University's objective of excellence in research, scholarship,
and education by publishing worldwide in

Oxford New York

Auckland Bangkok Buenos Aires Cape Town Chennai
Dar es Salaam Delhi Hong Kong Istanbul Karachi Kolkata
Kuala Lumpur Madrid Melbourne Mexico City Mumbai Nairobi
São Paulo Shanghai Taipei Tokyo Toronto

Oxford is a registered trade mark of Oxford University Press
in the UK and in certain other countries

British Library Cataloguing in Publication Data available

ISBN 0 19 279133 8 (hardback)
ISBN 0 19 272570 X (paperback)

10 9 8 7 6 5 4 3 2 1

Printed in China

Another tiger was looking up
at him from under the water.

This was
worrying.

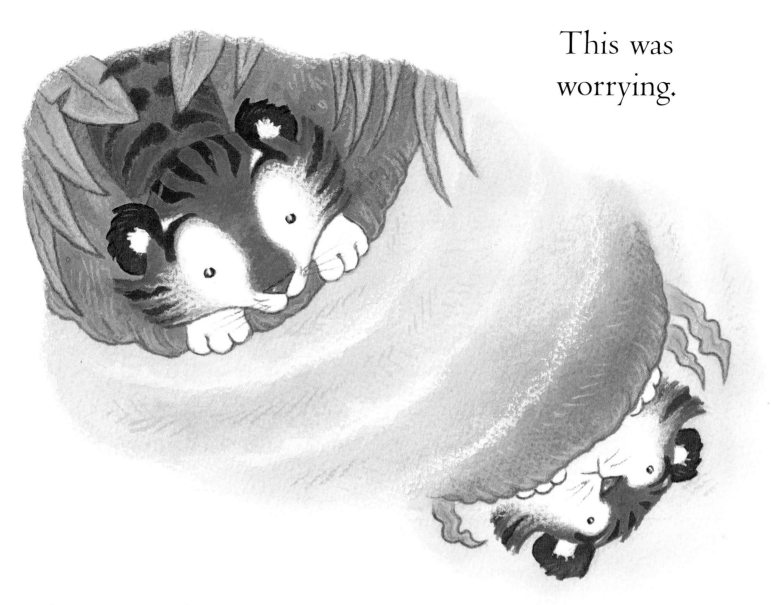

'Tigers can't swim!' cried Clovis.
'They NEVER go in the water!'

He ran to find something to
help the other tiger get out.

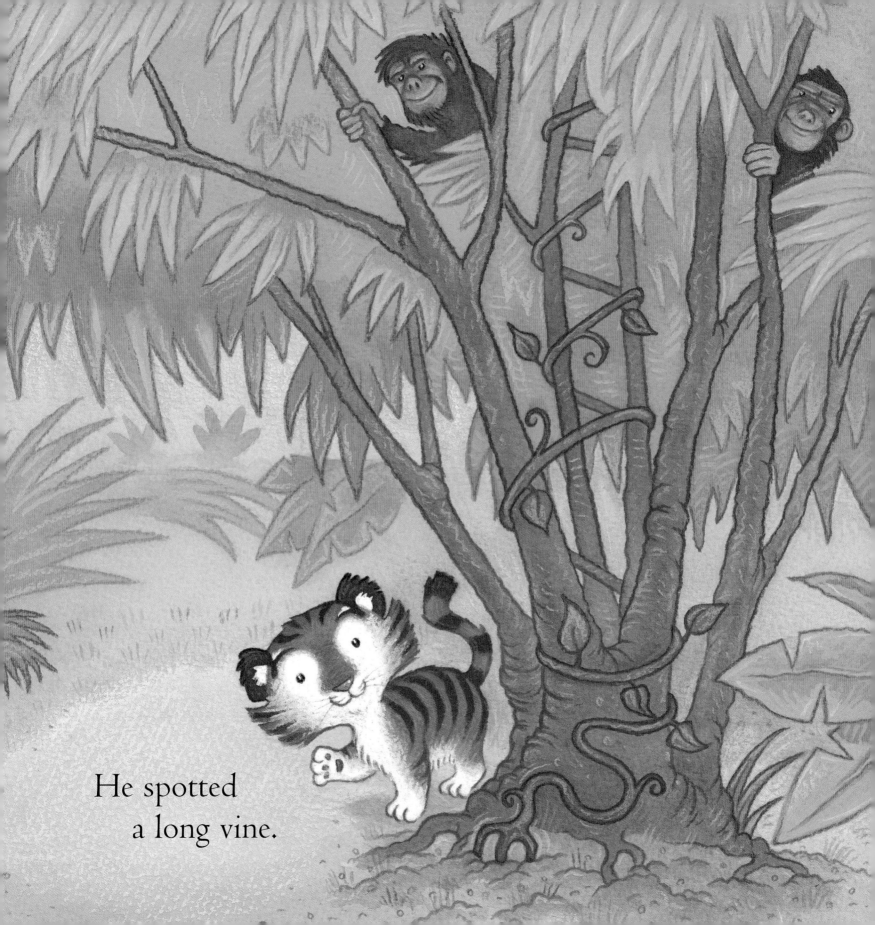

He spotted
a long vine.

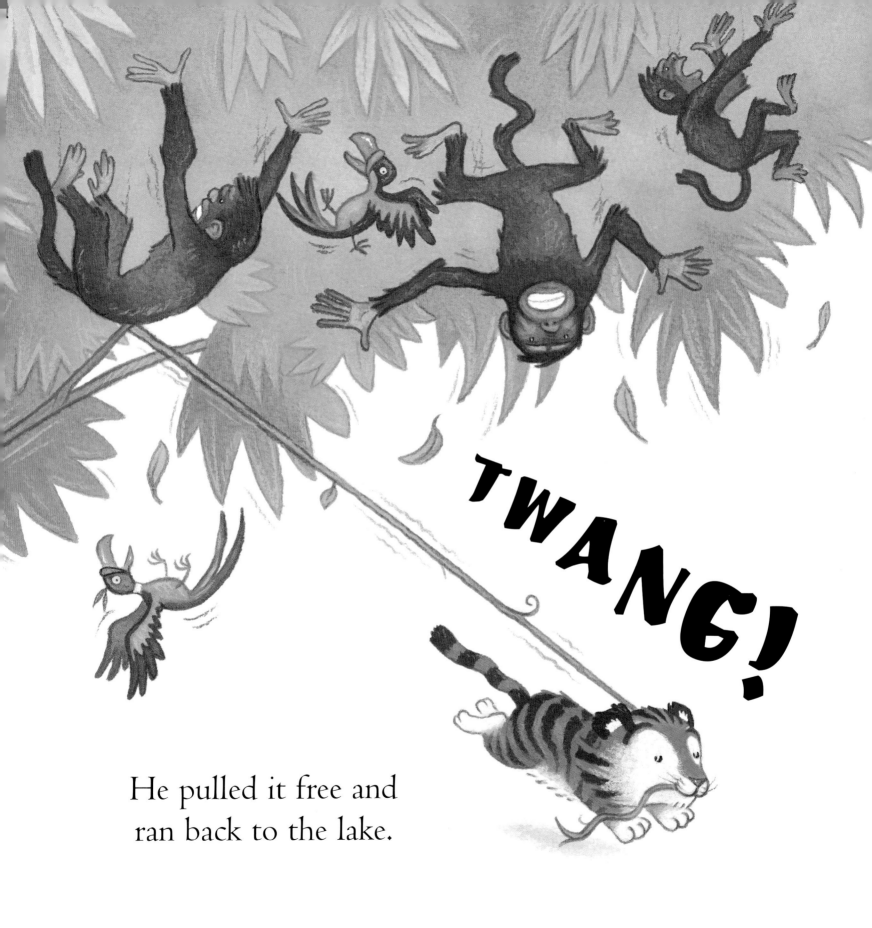

TWANG!

He pulled it free and
ran back to the lake.

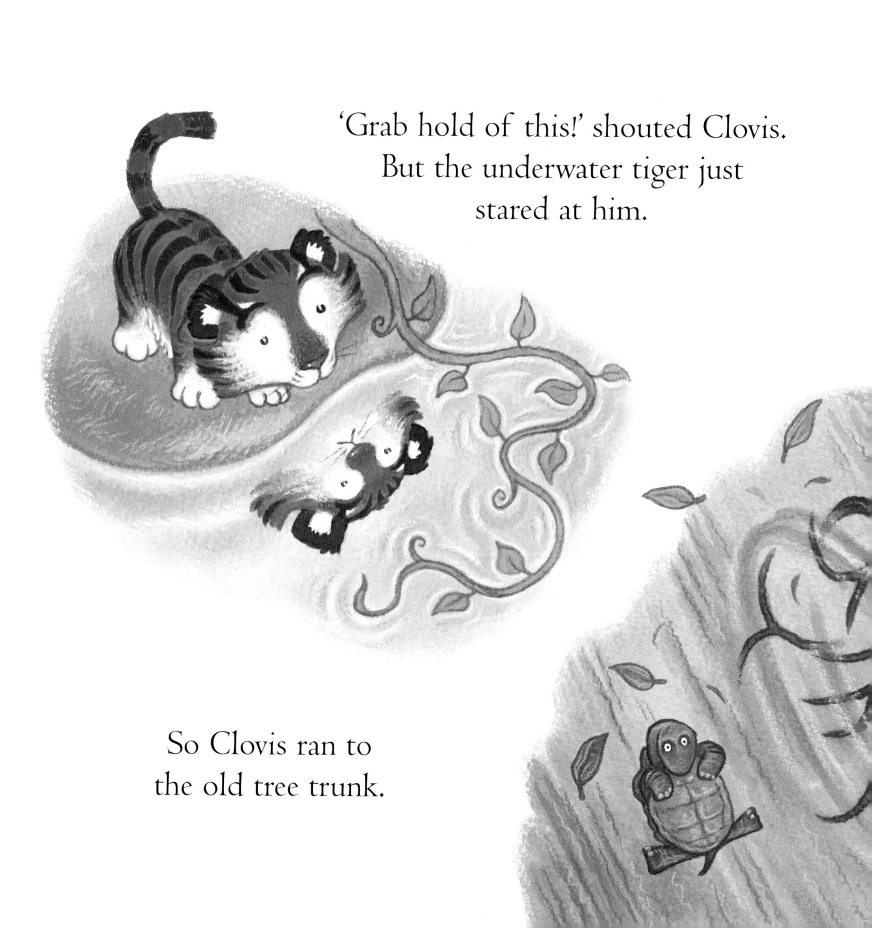

'Grab hold of this!' shouted Clovis.
But the underwater tiger just
stared at him.

So Clovis ran to
the old tree trunk.

RUMBLE!

He rolled it **down** to the lake.

SPLASH!

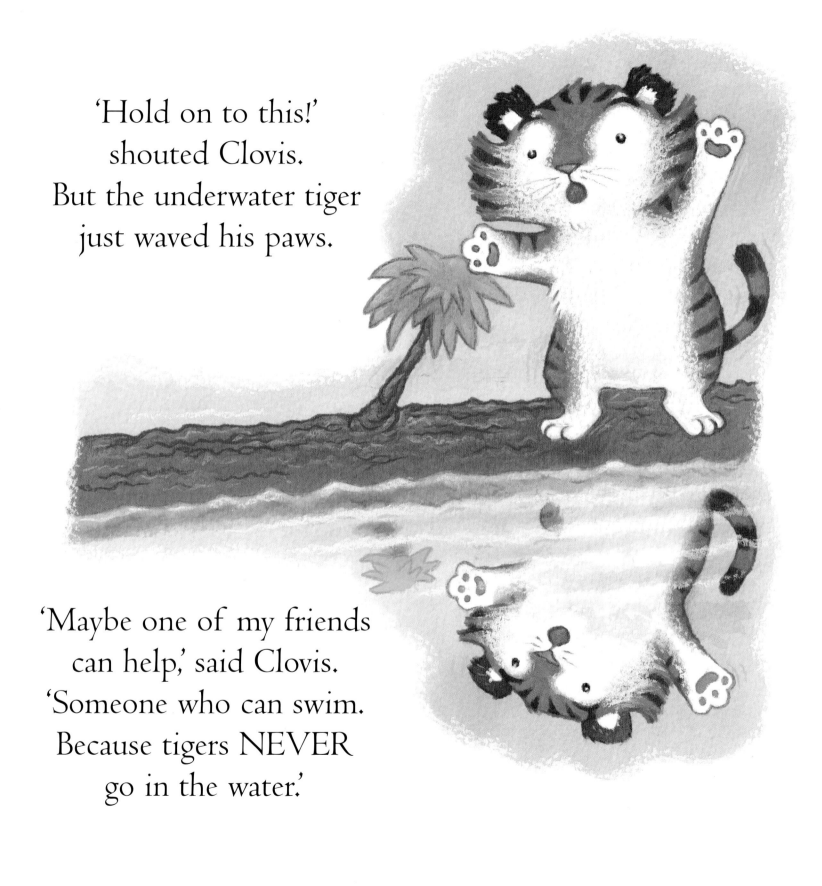

'Hold on to this!'
shouted Clovis.
But the underwater tiger
just waved his paws.

'Maybe one of my friends
can help,' said Clovis.
'Someone who can swim.
Because tigers NEVER
go in the water.'

His friend, Hortense, was enjoying a peaceful
wallow when — **sploosh sploosh sploosh** —
there was Clovis.

'Help!' he said. 'There's a tiger trapped under the water.
And tigers can't swim!'
'Now, Clovis,' said Hortense. 'I'm sure there isn't
really a tiger under the water.'

Sploosh!

'There is!'
shouted Clovis.
'Look!'

Hortense stuck her head under the water.
'No tigers down here,'
she bubbled.

Clovis leant over.
   'But there is a tiger,' he said.
               'A really frightened one!'

'Now, Clovis,' said Hortense. 'Don't get upset.
Why don't you jump in and rescue him yourself?'

'Me?'
said Clovis.
'But tigers can't swim!'

'Brave tigers can,'
said Hortense.

Clovis knew what
he had to do.

He took a deep breath,
closed his eyes, and...

SPLOOOSH!

It was the **biggest** splash he had ever made.

Down,

down,

down,

went Clovis, right to the bottom of the water.
He opened his eyes.
There was no underwater tiger to be seen.

Clovis bobbed back up.
'I'm floating!' he said.
'But where's the
underwater tiger?'

'Clovis, it was you,'
said Hortense.
'Me?'

'Yes, you. It was just your
reflection,' Hortense explained kindly.
'Now kick your legs and you'll be able to swim.'

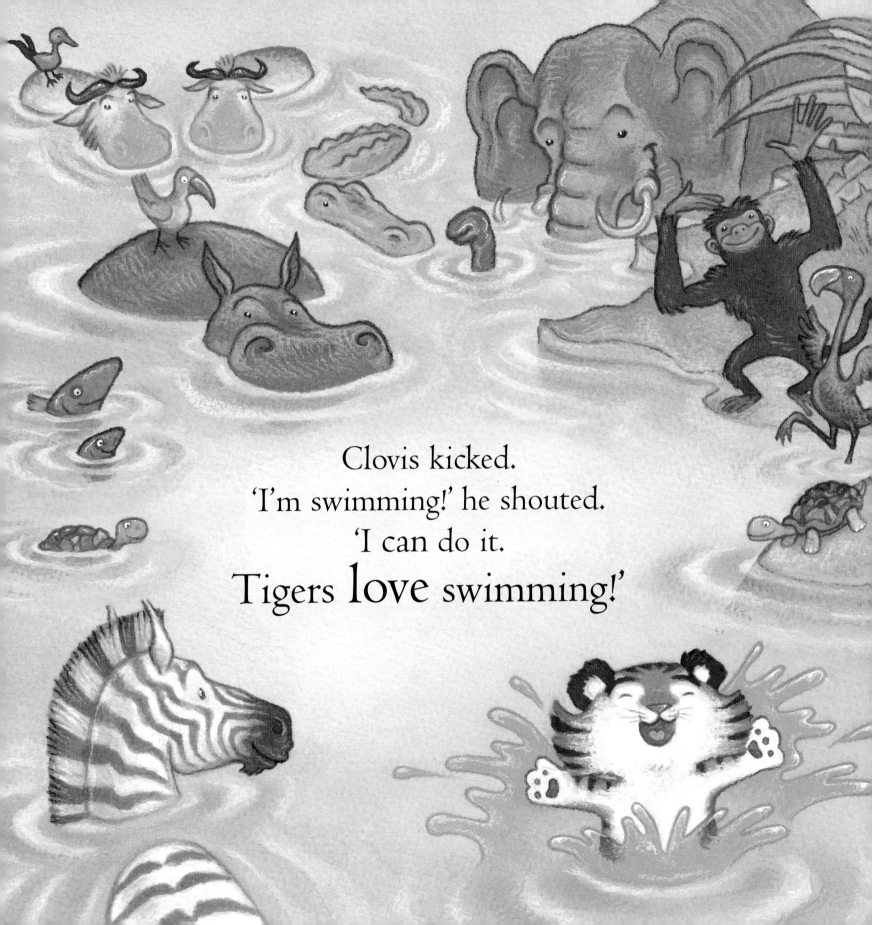

Clovis kicked.
'I'm swimming!' he shouted.
'I can do it.
Tigers love swimming!'

And everyone loved swimming with Clovis . . .

. . . most of the time.